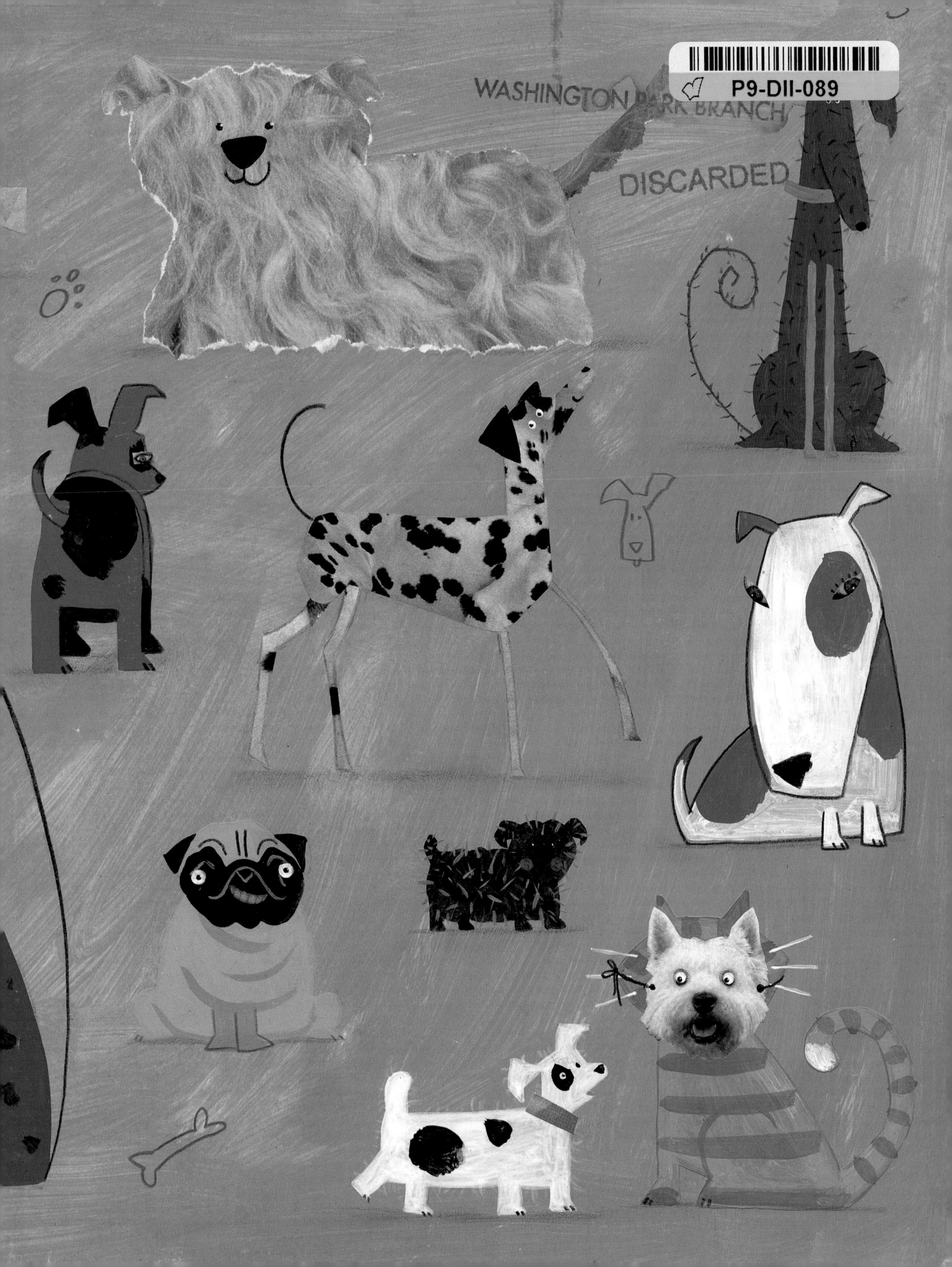

For
Simon, Bobbin, and Tess

First published in the United States 1999
by Dial Books for Young Readers
A member of Penguin Putnam Inc.
375 Hudson Street
New York, New York 10014

Published in Great Britain 1998
by Reed Children's Books as I Wish I Were a Dog
Copyright © 1998 by Lydia Monks
All rights reserved
Design and typography by Claire Harvey

Printed in UAE on acid-free paper
First Edition

1 3 5 7 9 10 8 6 4 2

Library of Congress Cataloging-in-Publication Data

Monks, Lydia.
The cat barked?/story and pictures by Lydia Monks.-1st ed.
p.   cm.
Summary: A cat that imagines life would be better as a dog recognizes,
after some thought, the many advantages of being a feline.
ISBN 0-8037-2338-5
[1. Cat-Fiction.   2. Dogs-Fiction.   3. Self-acceptance-Fiction.
4. Stories in rhyme.]   I. Title.
PZ8.3.M746Cat–1999–[E]-dc21–98-10134–CIP–AC

THE CAT BARKED?

LYDIA MONKS

Dial Books for Young Readers

New York

I wish I were a dog.
Dogs have all the fun!

If I were a dog,
I'd go to the park.

I'd throw back my head
And howl and bark.

Dogs guard the house,
They can catch crooks,

**And they're always the heroes
In movies and books.**

I wish *I* were a dog!

**Silly old cat,
If your wish did come true,**

You'd have to do things You *wouldn't* want to do.

Dogs have to eat bones

And do endless tricks.

They're always on leashes

And have to fetch sticks.

**A cat can do things
No dog ever could!**

Cats catch their own supper

And see in the dark.

**They're whispery quiet,
With no need to bark.**

Cats jump high in the air

And scramble up trees.

They can pounce like a tiger

And go where they please.

In sunny spots and soft places
Cats like to take naps,
And they're just the right size
For cuddling in laps.

If you were a dog,
You couldn't do that.
Please, stay just as you are –
A most wonderful cat.